MOLLY LIKOVICH

Riding The Headless Horseman

Contents

Playlist

❧

Gimme! Gimme! Gimme! by ABBA
A Dangerous Thing by AURORA
Take Me Home Tonight by Eddie Money
Meet Me in the Woods by Lord Huron
The Night We Met by Lord Huron
You're Dead by Norma Tanega
Halloween by Phoebe Bridgers
Villainous Thing by Shayfer James
willow by Taylor Swift
When I Met You from Lazarus the musical
Bedspell by Zolita
Heads Will Roll by Yeah Yeah Yeahs
Season of the Witch Lana Del Rey cover
Into the Unknown from Over The Garden Wall
Like Real People Do by Hozier
It's Called : Freefall Paris Paloma cover
Soldier, Poet, King by The Oh Hellos
Quietly Yours by Birdy
This Is Halloween izzy reign cover
The Four Horsemen by Metallica

Turn the Lights Off by Tally Hall
Witches by Alice Phoebe Lou
Mary on a Cross by Ghost
The Headless Horseman by Kay Starr
The Headless Horseman Dheusta cover
Headless Horseman by William Allen Jones

LISTEN TO THE PLAYLIST HERE:
https://music.apple.com/us/playlist/riding-the-headless-horseman/pl.u-d2b0KdlTBlVMA

Artwork by River Meade

CONTENT WARNING

This book contains explicit sexual content including dubcon, spanking, light BDSM, bloodplay, choking, and waxplay. Also contains mentions of past emotional and physical abuse. It is intended for readers 18+ so please proceed with caution.

For River, my fellow monster lover.

And my mother for supporting this insanity.

"'Faith, sir,' replied the storyteller, 'as to that matter, I don't believe one half of it myself.'"

-The Legend of Sleepy Hollow

One

All Hallows' Eve

L et it hereby be known that I, Arletta Harrington, do not
believe in Death.

   To be clear, I believe in *dying,* I'm not a fool. I just
don't believe in the physical, humanoid, embodiment of death
that plagues our many forms of fiction. Take your pick of any
of the 'Deaths' there have been on page and screen; Death in
Gaiman's *Sandman* series, the Reaper from *The Grim Adventures
of Billy & Mandy,* Death in *The Book Thief;* all nice stories, some
more meaningful than others, but when it comes to the idea
that Death is a man or woman walking around our world I
don't believe a lick of it.

   I know what you're thinking: 'Arletta no one believes in those,
they're all so clearly fake.' Not where I live, they're not.

   At least not the idea—the legend that inspired them all.

   Here in Sleepy Hollow, most folks believe Death to be
a walking, talking person who comes into our town every

Autumn to terrorize those left lurking the streets late at night. Whenever someone dies in October it's chalked up to his handiwork, never what it actually is. Like sickness, or infection. Hell, I once saw a guy I used to date die in a car crash and his family still claimed that Death had a hand in it.

Or, well, not 'Death' that's not what we call him—not what *they* call him (remember? I don't believe in all that nonsense).

The Headless Horseman.

That's his name.

Some drunk colonial guy raved about it in a tavern centuries ago and the legend has stuck like gum to a shoe ever since.

And according to the legend, tonight is *his* night.

Halloween, baby.

But it's also *my* night. Being a witch pays in a town hellbent on adamantly proclaiming the existence of spooks. This is why I've had a line of customers outside my cottage all evening waiting for one of my readings.

I do them all: tarot, crystals, palm, pendulum, ruins, you name it. I'm partial to tarot. It was my nana's favorite form of divination. Every time I dust off her old deck to give myself a little reading, I always feel a bit closer to her.

But that deck is strictly for me. No amount of money would ever sway me to let anyone else talk me into giving them a reading from it. No, my customers have a variety of decks to choose from that range from the classic Ryder Waite, to more kitschy ones like The Everyday Witch. I even have a few movie-themed decks; Alice in Wonderland, Labyrinth, I even have a Jane Austen deck (it's not very accurate, it thinks we're all going to be spinsters. But I *am* 28 and unwed so by Austen standards I suppose it's right).

Samantha Waverly, the town herbalist, sits across from me

with eager eyes as I turn the last card of her reading over.

"Two of cups."

"What does that mean?" She asks as she twists her fingers anxiously, popping a few knuckles in the process. "Is he the one for me?"

"You have a strong emotional bond. Build upon that."

"But—" she frowns a bit. Oh god, she's one of *those* kinds of customers. "Is he my soulmate?"

I fight the overwhelming urge to roll my eyes.

"You know I don't believe in soulmates, Samantha."

"Maybe the cards think differently than you."

I pause for a moment and her eyes light up, clearly thinking she's convinced me to give her a different outcome (as if I could, not how tarot works, folks).

"Nope," I say as I swipe the cards back into the deck. "That'll be $30."

She grumbles under her breath as she fishes two twenties out of her bag.

"Keep the change," she says, standing up. "Happy Halloween, Letta."

"Thanks, you too."

* * *

I walk her to the door, double-check that I don't have any more customers, then lock it and head back into my office. My 'office' is the room I use for my public magic. Where I perform readings and peddle my wares: crystals, spell pouches, and potions that won't do any of the things I claim that they will. My magic in

3

this room is half real and half show. Because most people don't want *real* magic. They don't want the grit and grime that comes along with such an arcane practice. Their hearts can't handle the darkness that even the brightest magic can cause.

So I play it by ear, feeling out each customer to see who wants that real, intense, true witch work and who wants the showy, hocus pocus, double double toil, and trouble nonsense. And through this keen sense of customer evaluation, I'm able to pay my bills and keep the lights on all while avoiding a nine to five.

Not bad. Not bad at all.

The small room behind my office is just for me.

It's where I conduct *my* magic.

The spells and secrets I save just for me.

I enter and get started on my own Samhain work. I cleanse the room with dragon's blood incense and then I carefully place crystals along the tiny windowsill—each one blessed with water charged under the last full moon. I light several white, vanilla-scented, tea light candles, even placing one inside a cute little Jack-O-Lantern holder, and then I light the tall black candle in the center of my altar. I sit on the plush pillow in front of it and produce my nana's tarot deck from a pocket in my black cardigan.

I kept it on my person all day. I just wanted to feel close to her. She was the only other witch in my family. My parents died young and my aunt rejected the whole practice. No siblings. No magic-thirsty cousins, not even a best friend to share the art of the arcane with. Just Nana and me.

Now just me.

Even in a town as macabre and flat-out weird as Sleepy Hollow, everyone still wants to paint at least one person as the outcast. The odd one. The crazy one. The witch of the

4

wood.

I only live at the edge of the forest, but you get the idea.

First, my nana was the village crazy lady, and post-college I took up the mantle after her death.

I don't regret a thing.

Well, in regards to magic anyway.

The only thing Nana and I disagreed on was Death. She believed in The Headless Horseman as much as any other Sleepy Hollow Head. We argued about it. I would tell her how it went against all of our other beliefs to think that the deity of Death was some New Yorker (sans head) on a horse.

I won the argument when she died on a cold October night four years ago. I watched the life leave her body and no Horseman came in to whisk her away.

The Horseman is a relic of times gone by. He doesn't belong in the here and now.

And in the here and now it's almost the Witching Hour and I can't let my grief cloud my work. The Veil between the worlds will only be this thin until the sun rises tomorrow, and I want Nana's guidance. I want to speak to her the only way I know how.

Magic.

Divination.

Tarot.

Nana would use the cards to commune with her childhood love every Samhain (even before my Grandpapi died), so I use them every year to try and receive divine intervention from her.

I shuffle her cards, savoring the familiar feel of the worn-down edges against my fingertips. I close my eyes and let the cards speak to me. When I open my eyes three cards have fallen

5

from the deck and onto my altar. I flip them over one by one.

Four of Pentacles.

Stressed about money and fear of lack of stability. Yeah, Nana, I know. Tell me something new.

The Hermit.

Not as judgmental as it sounds. I look at the woman in a deep, purple cape, finding her way out of a dark cave by the light of her lantern. I need to trust myself to see myself through. Through what? I have no idea.

I flip over the last card.

The Lovers.

Now that's a good joke, Nana. Hilarious. A lover hasn't dared to darken my doorway since Ethan.

(If Nana had still been alive when I dated Ethan he would've become the second thing we disagreed on, and she would've been the one in the right.)

Maybe it's for the best.

At least that's what I tell myself.

I put the cards back in the deck, feeling a little dejected. I always hope for some great prophecy, but when I read for myself that never seems to work out. The cards read more like a to-do list or a motivational piece of wall art than anything close to true divination. It's too late to do any truly complicated and intricate spellwork, and my magical battery is thoroughly drained from selling readings all night.

I decide to go for a walk; let the starry sky bring me back to life.

* * *

The New York October air nips at my nose and I really wish I had thought to grab a coat. Instead, I'm walking the streets in nothing but my black, wool cardigan, and a flimsy white nightgown. I look like I stepped right off the cover of a cheesy, dime-back gothic romance.

Well, it is Halloween after all, may as well give the village folk a show so they have something to gossip about in the school carpool lane tomorrow.

'Did you see Arletta Harrington last night? Walking around in nothing but her nightgown!'

'Probably sacrificing animals to the Devil.'

Thank god I wasn't alive in the 17th century. Hell, even if I was alive in the 80s the Satanic Panic would've for sure landed my ass in jail.

Just the thought of witch persecution makes me feel nervous. Another rough wind blows and I pull my cardigan tighter around my body as I make my way toward the town bridge. The deeper part of the forest lies beyond. Most people are afraid to go there. Some for typical forest-based fears, others because they believe it to be Death's domain.

Sure, Karen. Sure.

I reach the edge of the bridge and feel something brush against my side from within my pocket. I reach in and pull out whatever it is.

A tarot card

Death.

I look up over the bridge and see a looming shadow at the other end. I take a step back, suddenly feeling like the biggest idiot in the world for coming out here alone. Idiot horror movie maiden— party of one.

The wind howls and with it, a deep, rumbling voice speaks.

"Come to me."

Okay, not loving this at all.

I take another step back.

The shadow moves.

Hell no.

I turn and run.

Two

Death

She runs from me.

They always run.

But I could smell the witching on her from miles away. Her heady

magic scent carried across the treetops and into my domain. Across the Bone Bridge and over my Moors.

I felt her.

My soulless body craves her body, so full of life and passion. She is more soulful than any other creature in this pitiful excuse for a town.

She runs from me, but now that I've got her scent, she will never be able to hide.

Three

The Witching Hour

Y*ou're an idiot, Arletta,* is what I keep telling myself over and over as I race down the dirt road that leads from the outskirts of town. I can hear the shadow creature behind me.

I can hear...hoofs.

No.

No freaking way.

My chest burns from all the running; the cold night air working against me. I stop for just a moment to catch my breath and attempt to process what's happening. I turn back and only have a moment to make any sense of what I'm seeing before The Horseman gallops towards me with a vengeance, reaches out with one arm, and hoists me up over his horse, the shadowy beast not once missing a single stride.

I open my mouth to scream but my stomach hits the saddle hard and all the air gets knocked out of me. The Horseman keeps a large, gloved hand, pressed firmly to my back, keeping me pinned horizontally across the still galloping horse.

After a few moments I'm able to breathe somewhat normally again, so I open my mouth and scream.

My scream is nowhere near as loud as I'd like. I don't sound at all like a slasher movie final girl but more the doomed gothic lady I'm dressed as.

"Be quiet now," the voice from the bridge says. The voice is gritty. From this close vicinity, I can hear a slight accent that I can't quite identify. It's not American, that much I know.

I try to look up at The Horseman and confirm what I already know to be true.

He. Is. Headless.

Well…

There *is* something sitting on his shoulders but it's not a head. It's a glowing Jack-O-Lantern. The face carved into it is a wicked one and the candle burns ferociously bright. But the mouth doesn't move as the voice speaks. The bridge voice that obviously must somehow be his.

"We are almost there," he says.

Great, I feel so much better now.

I realize I should probably be fighting this abduction. That's what a sane person would do. But then again a sane person probably wouldn't go walking around alone in the dark near the part of town where centuries of residents have sworn up and down is the home of the Harbinger of Death.

I try to squirm and kick against his impossibly strong hand keeping me pinned to this freaking horse.

To no avail.

"Stop moving, little mortal. I do not wish to punish you. Just obey me."

Oh absolutely not.

I try to scream again and I swear I can hear him groan. He digs his fingers into my back, gripping the fabric of my sweater in his hand as he yanks me up to sitting. He swings one of my legs to the other side of the horse so that I'm straddling the four-legged beast with my back pressed up against him.

He wraps the same arm that was keeping me pinned down a moment ago, around my waist, pulling me as close to his body as he can. His grip on me is firm and panic is finally starting to sink in.

I've been abducted.

By an urban legend.

"Let me go," I say, softly, as gently as I can manage in my state of quickly growing terror and anger, "please."

"No."

Great. Great chat.

I wriggle against him and in doing so I feel something push against my lower back.

Oh.

Oh.

He may not be endowed with a head but he clearly makes up for it in...*other* departments.

Out of all the things I would've guessed this malevolent presence (that evidently has been plaguing our town for centuries) would want to do with me, getting it on would've been very low on the list.

I assumed beings like him wanted to suck souls or something. I don't know. Feast on my brains? No, he's not a zombie. Though he is lacking a brain. Right? No head must equal no brain.

Jesus my thoughts are racing as fast as this god-forsaken hell-horse.

I look around me as the trees blur past me, becoming shadows themselves. We ride across the bridge and deep into the forest. I give up trying to get free from his grasp, it's impossible. But the deeper we go the more terrified I become.

I do not recognize these trees.

They look wrong somehow. A little too bent. A little too gaunt. A little too *ghostly*.

I see another bridge in the distance and as we get closer I feel my heart drop into my stomach. The bridge is made of *bones.*

The hell-horse clip-clops across it and we are in a world made up of darkness.

The stars are the only light.

The air stinks of death and decay.

The wind doesn't blow and yet it's somehow colder than it was on the other side of the bridge.

This is the land of the dead.

That's where I am right now.

I press my hand to my heart. It's still beating. I breathe a small sigh of relief.

"Come, little mortal. We're home."

Home? I don't think so. Not a chance in hell. Or…a chance in here.

The Horseman gets down and reaches out, grabbing my waist and hauling me down after him. I yelp softly as I practically crash into his arms. I try to shove him away, pushing against the thick fabric of the black cloak he wears, but he just holds my forearms tightly and refuses to allow me freedom of movement.

"Stop that now," he says.

I go still. His voice no longer sounds like thunder caught in someone's throat. It is still deep and powerful, but it sounds like it's coming from an actual, living person.

He must (somehow) notice (seriously, how? He doesn't have eyes, just a freaking pumpkin head) my realization.

"I can speak clearer here in my realm. It is easier to make my thoughts into words you can hear and understand."

Okayyyyy…so he's thinking at me?

"I'd like to go home now," I whisper.

He slides his hands down my arms to grasp my hands in his large, gloved ones. "You are home. Now come."

He begins to drag me towards a cave. I quickly dig my heels into the dirt and try to resist. But I'm wearing a flimsy pair of flats and he has supernatural strength on his side. After a few failed attempts I end up falling forward, crashing to the ground. He releases my hands only to scoop me up, throwing me over his shoulder.

"No!" I shout, fighting to have some kind of autonomy here. "Put me down!" He spanks me. *Hard.* I cry out from the sudden, and unfamiliar pain.

"Behave, little mortal. I told you I do not want to punish you, but I will."

Everything in me is telling me to keep fighting him. But instead, I go slack in his arms and let him carry me to the cave.

We enter and it's nothing like I thought it would be. Instead of some damp, craggy enclosure, it's like the foyer of a mansion, only everything is made of bone and stone.

He keeps going, until he reaches the center of this foyer-like room and deposits me on a black, plush sofa.

He stands before me. The stone bone foyer is lit only by candles but it's bright enough for me to fully drink in the sight before me. And it is nightmarish.

An eight-foot-tall man clad all in black, muscles so big that his clothes stretch taut across his body, and nothing but that goddamn pumpkin on his shoulders.

"Are you going to behave, little mortal?"

"Arletta."

"Hmm?"

"My name," I clarify, "isn't *little mortal,* it's Arletta. Or Letta if you're my friend—which you most certainly are not—but if you want me to behave then call me by my name."

I want to say that he smirks. But of course, he doesn't. But it...*feels* like he's smirking at me. Can he think facial expressions at me too the same way he can think his side of the conversation aloud?

Not that this has been much of a conversation.

"Very well, Arletta. Are you going to behave?"

"Are you going to kill me if I don't?" My hand flies to my chest again to make sure I can still feel my heart beating under my skin.

"I don't want you dead," he says. "I like you alive."

"Oh good. Me too."

He think-smirks at me again.

"I told you, I will punish you if you do not behave but I will not kill you."

"I thought that's what you did. Kill people."

"And why would you think that, Arletta?"

"Well...aren't you..." my voice trails off. I just can't even fully comprehend that this moment is occurring.

(Could you? No. Who could? No one, that's who.)

"Who is it that you think I am?"

"Death."

"I work for Death, but I am not them."

"Oh," I say. "But the stories say—"

15

"You are an inquisitive one, my Arletta."

"I'm not *your* Arletta."

"Not yet. But you will be. You will see. Fear can turn to love."

"What?" I say in disbelief. "What are you talking about? What do you want?"

"I thought that was rather obvious. I want you. And I intend to have you."

Then he reaches up and removes the Jack-O-Lantern from his shoulders and places it on a nearby table.

"Don't you…" I sputter, taken aback by the sight of him *truly* devoid of a head. It's even more disturbing than when he was sporting a gourd in place of an actual skull. "Don't you need that to see?"

"I do not think of sight the same way that you do, Arletta. The pumpkin helps me see clearly in your realm. Here in my realm, I do not need it. I am freer without it."

"Okay," I whisper.

He leans over me. I have no idea where to look. There is nothing to look at. So I close my eyes.

He trails a hand down the column of my throat and I inhale softly.

"Mmm, yes, Arletta. I will make you mine. I knew it from the very first moment I sensed you."

I say nothing. He removes his hand. I open my eyes to see him begin to slowly peel away his gloves and toss them aside. His hands look like they're made up of shadows. His skin seems almost translucent, like it's made up of the night sky and stars as opposed to flesh and blood.

He extends the same hands back and begins to stroke the other side of my neck, gently toying with the spot just below my ear. And I can't help it. I sigh.

It feels good.

And it's been a very long time since I've felt good.

Ethan made me feel somewhat good once upon a time. But that soured quickly. His goodness was a pretty mask he wore to get me to bed. His rough touches quickly became fists and thrown plates. I sent him packing and vowed loneliness was safer than risking heartbreak over a violent man.

The Headless Horseman is hardly a man.

"Give in to me, Arletta," he says. "Just obey me. It will free you."

"To obey you?"

"Yes," he practically purrs as he leans his headless body down over mine.

He moves his shadowy hand down my throat and dips down into my clavicle and across my collarbone. He's exerting the lightest, most feathery touches and somehow it's driving me more insane than if he were being rough with me.

"Doesn't it feel good, little mortal?"

He traces his hand down lower until he reaches the hem of my nightgown.

"Arletta," I say around a sigh. "Call me by name or nothing at all."

He chuckles.

Without a head, let alone a mouth, *he chuckles.*

It doesn't sound condescending though, it sounds almost sweet.

"Doesn't it feel good, Arletta?"

He gently tugs my nightgown down so that my breasts spill out.

"Beautiful," The Horseman murmurs.

He traces his hands gently down the top of my left breast.

17

"Answer me," he commands as he gently pinches my nipple. I inhale sharply again.

"Yes," I answer. "It feels good."

He continues to tweak and pinch at my left nipple until it puckers and stands erect. Then he proceeds to do the same to the right. I want him to torture both at once—badly. But it's clear he's the kind of lover whose foreplay can last for hours.

"What do I call you?" I whisper, growing breathless, my eyes still closed.

"Master."

I open my eyes.

"Absolutely not."

He pinches my nipples—hard, just like his spank from earlier. I gasp, shocked by how quickly his gentle ministrations can turn to more violent forms of passion.

"Yes," he practically hisses. "I told you, Arletta, you are mine. You must submit to me. It will free you."

"That sounds like the opposite of freedom."

He twists my nipples and I can't help but groan.

"Oh but it is. Every day you carry around the weight of that cursed town. The hateful glances of those mortals who lack your magic. Your witch work hangs around you like a beautiful shadow. But you peddle it for profit, and the ones who buy it show you no respect."

"How do you know all that?"

"I am a messenger of Death, I can see the lifelines all around the souls I claim. Most souls I take are wicked, some are merely annoying or tiresome. But you—" he tugs on my nipples, moving me forward. Without thinking my hands go out in front of me and press against his firm chest. "—*you*, I took because of how vibrant your soul is."

18

"What happens to the people you take? You deliver them to Death?"

He finally releases my breasts and begins tugging my nightgown down further to expose my stomach.

"Yes."

"But you're not taking me to Death?"

He digs his nails into my stomach.

"No, I told you I would not and I always keep my word. You are mine now and I intend to keep you."

He straightens back to standing at his full height and I would say he looks down at me but...well, you know.

"Stand," he says, "undress."

I remain seated, tits out, before The Headless Horseman. Weirdest Halloween yet, that's for sure.

"Arletta, I told you to obey me."

"And if I don't?"

"Then I will punish you."

I stare at him for a moment, my mind thinking back to the spanking and pinching. He's serious. And if those weren't punishments I can only imagine what the real deal looks like with a creature like him.

I stand up and slowly remove my sweater, nightgown, and lastly, my underwear.

I stand before him, completely bare.

"Well," I whisper, "can you even...can you even really see me?"

He steps closer to me, reaches down, and takes my face in his hands.

"Yes, Arletta, I can see every piece of you."

"How?" I ask. "You're not wearing the...the pumpkin." God, that sounds ridiculous.

"I told you I do not need it here, in my realm."

"Then how? How does that work? How can you see me here?"

"I see your beauty because I feel it. It radiates off of you louder than your magic."

"That's so weird," I whisper, unable to help it.

He chuckles again.

"Perhaps. I can see how it would be to a mortal. But you will get used to it eventually. Unfortunately, I have been alone for a long time and I am too impatient to wait for you to become familiar with my form."

"Impatient to…"

"Claim you."

"Oh. By having sex I assume?"

He suddenly dips a hand between my thighs and I gasp again. I feel slightly appalled to realize how wet I am.

I'm aroused by a monster from legend.

Figures.

"Yes," Arletta," he growls. "I have every intention of fucking you relentlessly tonight."

I open my mouth to respond but he inserts two fingers into me and I cry out in surprise, grabbing his arms tightly and pressing my head against his chest.

"Yes," he murmurs, "give in to me."

He begins to pump his fingers in and out of me, fucking me with his hand. I moan again and nuzzle into his chest.

"That's it," he says, using his other hand to smooth down my hair, "give in."

I do.

I absolutely do.

He finger fucks me harder and harder until I'm so close I feel like I might burst.

Then he removes his fingers abruptly, I cry out from the

20

horrible hollow, empty feeling that follows, but it only lasts a moment before he pinches my clit between his thumb and forefinger. I have never had any lover do that to me and the sensation is overwhelmingly, beautifully painful.

"Yes," he whispers into my hair. "Come now."

And then he slaps my clit just as hard as he did my ass earlier. I scream into his chest and he holds me tightly as the orgasm rushes through my body.

That was the most intense sexual experience I've ever had and he hasn't even properly fucked me yet.

I press my hands flat against his chest.

"Tell me who you truly are," I whisper. "Tell me your story and then I will fully submit to you."

"Alright, Arletta."

Four

Hessian

I t has been so long since I've spoken to anyone but Death. So long since a human has greeted me with anything but screams of terror. The sound of a soul heavy with guilt.

But not Arletta.

She did not scream until I made her climax.

As nervous as she may be by my monstrous stature, she is not afraid, not truly.

And even so...

Fear can turn to love.

So I will tell her what I have never told another soul.

I will tell her who I am.

Five

The Legend of Sleepy Hollow

" I assume if you want me to stay with you forever you are aware that as a mortal, I need to eat and drink."

"Yes, Arletta, I am aware. I can procure you sustenance."

"What about… wine?" I venture.

He laughs and pushes a lock of hair behind my ear.

It's still somewhat disorienting to be conversing with a voice I can't truly see the source of. I know it's technically coming from him. From his thoughts. But come on—wouldn't you too struggle with the concept of having a discussion with someone who's lacking a head?

"Yes, I can bring you wine."

I say nothing. He laughs again then retreats to another room of his bone mansion. I look around then awkwardly sit back down on the sofa. I'm tempted to put my clothes back on but *Master* didn't say I could so despite how somewhat stupid I find the notion of calling anyone that, I'm not ready to have any of my sensitive areas spanked again.

He returns with a large, silver goblet full of red wine and hands it to me. I take a small sip, it's the most delicious wine I've ever tasted.

"Are you ready?" He asks.

"Yes."

"Very well. The year was 1790, I had just arrived in America."

"From where?" I ask.

"Hesse."

"Your accent," I say. "It's German? It sounds...older."

"I would imagine it does. About 300 years older."

"Yeah," I say, softly. Feeling a bit silly. "So...you came to Sleepy Hollow from Hesse. Then what?"

"Long version or short version?"

"Well you don't need to spin me a Homeric epic, but I don't want a vague metaphor of an answer either."

He laughs again—softer this time. Then a more solemn energy sinks into his disembodied voice.

"I was accused of witchcraft and hanged. As a witch of The Hollow you may or may not be aware of the fact that back then witches were decapitated after they were hanged as a way to make sure Satan did not raise them from the dead."

"Oh god."

He sits down next to me on the sofa and places his hand on my bare thigh. He begins to slowly drag his nails back and forth, sending electricity all throughout my skin.

"There is no god. Not like that."

"Is Death a god?"

"In a way."

"And you work for him? Why didn't you...I don't know, move on? Wherever there is to go to. There is somewhere to go to,

24

right?"

"Yes. But I was not ready to go. I wanted to punish those who had wronged me."

"Surely all those puritans are dead now."

He drags his hand up and begins to slide it between my legs again. I instinctively part them.

"Yes. But evil never truly dies. You should know this. I can see darkness in your soul, but it's not yours. Someone put it there."

"Yes," I say. "Someone did."

Or many. Ethan. The people in town.

"Were you a witch?" I ask.

"No," he says. "Most of those who were hanged for it weren't. Witches were more clever at hiding than historians like to think."

I can't help but laugh. "And now we announce our presence and sell our services."

"Yes," he murmurs through what sounds like a smile that I know doesn't really exist.

He slides his fingers between my folds and I sigh.

"Is that why you want me?" I ask breathlessly. "Because I'm a witch?"

"No, Arletta," his voice whispers in my ear, leaning his body against mine as he drags his fingers slowly along the outside of my pussy; unabatedly teasing me. "Your soul is vibrant, startlingly so. I want you with or without your magic. I want you because I can see all of you and I can *feel* that you are meant to be my companion. My mate. I've isolated myself for a long time. That ends tonight."

His words are too heavy. Too powerful. Too meaningful. I should protest them and go back to fighting to leave…

But…

God, I wish I could *kiss* him.

He finally dips his fingers back inside me. I lean back and moan loudly as he laughs in an almost appreciative way as he continues to move his hand against me. I buck my hips and he grinds the heel of his hand against my clit as I do.

"Please," I whimper when he removes his fingers without providing me release.

"Please what, Arletta?"

"Please make me come."

He says nothing and his hand remains on the inside of my thigh. Much too far away from where I want it—where I *need* it.

"Please…Master."

A low rumble ghosts across the air, a sound more primal than a mortal man could make and it ignites a fire in me that no mortal man ever could.

He thrusts his fingers back inside me, pressing his thumb to my clit and circling it ferociously. I cry out and come violently, my whole body shaking.

Before my orgasm has even had a chance to finish racking my body with spasms, he scoops me into his arms and makes his way over to a staircase at the far end of the foyer, made from bones as white as fresh snow.

"Where are we going?" I murmur against his chest.

"I'm taking you to bed. I need to be inside you. I need to make you mine."

I don't argue.

He carries me into a large bedroom, a bed covered in black satin blankets and sheets sits in the center, surrounded by nothing but candles that float in the air, faintly glowing orange like the Jack-O-Lantern he wore in place of a head.

"Do you even sleep?" I ask as he carries me to the bed.

"Occasionally."

He sets me down on the bed, it's so soft it feels more like resting on a heavenly cloud than a mattress.

I watch with hungry eyes as he begins to remove his clothes. His cloak and 18th-century frock and ruffled shirt. His chest is chiseled and has the same shadowy quality to it that his hands do. He is very much *there,* a flesh and bone man before me, but there is an ethereal quality to his skin. Not quite a ghost, not quite alive. Forever in limbo between man and specter.

His hands go to his pants, he undoes the laces and lets them fall to the floor, his erection springing free.

My observation from atop his horse has proven correct.

He has the biggest cock I have ever seen.

It is long and thick, so much so that I worry it might just tear me in two. He somehow sees the hesitation on my face and brushes his knuckles along my cheek.

"I won't hurt you."

I lean into his touch.

"I believe you."

He climbs on top of me slowly, positioning himself between my legs. I'm going to take a wild guess that birth control isn't going to be an issue here. I never heard of anyone getting pregnant from an agent of doom and gloom.

"Spread your legs for me, Arletta."

I do as he says. He was right, there is a certain sense of freedom in obeying him; in letting go of my inhibitions and giving myself over to him completely. I feel more relaxed than I have in years.

He reaches a hand down to run his fingers along my folds

again. "You're soaking wet, Arletta. You will be able to take me easily."

With that, he begins to slide into me. I inhale sharply from the pressure of him filling me up so completely. His cock stretches me more than I ever have been and for a moment I don't think I'll be able to handle it.

"Breathe, Arletta."

I exhale slowly and let my muscles relax. He pushes in deeper and I groan as he buries his length deep inside me until he's fully settled between my legs.

"I'm going to move now," he says.

"Okay."

"I am not going to be gentle the first time," he warns.

The first time.

I nod. "Alright then."

He pulls back out to the tip and then slams into me, our bodies slapping together loudly. I lean back and cry out from the horribly, wonderful intensity of it.

He continues to slam in and out of me, my body moving in perfect rhythm with his, and I want so badly to scream his name but he hasn't given me one.

He hitches my legs up around his waist and begins to fuck me harder, his cock hitting a sweeter part inside me from this new angle. I groan even louder as his hips continue to piston against mine.

"Please," I moan. "Please make me come."

He slows his movements and I practically growl from frustration. He laughs. Cocky bastard.

"Try that again, my sweet thing."

"Please make me come, Master."

"Good girl."

He begins to fuck me hard again and I scream from the pleasure. He moves harder and faster than I ever thought was possible and my body takes it all. His voice makes a rumbling sound in the air as he finishes, his body slamming into me one final time.

He lets his body sink down on top of mine and I wrap my arms around his back, and god do I wish I could kiss him now more than ever.

We lay like that for a few moments. Then he straightens back up and stands, he holds a hand out to me.

"Come, Arletta," he says. "Let's have a bath."

* * *

The bathroom made of stone and bone is just as stunning as the rest of his mansion. It's more like a lavish bathhouse than a regular bathroom. The large bathing pool is lined by more floating candles like the ones in the bedroom, and the ceiling shimmers like it's made of starlight. Who knew a world made of death could hold so much beauty?

We settle into the bath on one of the stone benches that runs along the side. He reaches for some soap that rests on the side and begins to create a lather in his hands.

"I can wash myself," I say.

"I don't care," he replies, and then his hands are on my body again.

He begins to scrub the soap across my shoulders, my breasts, and my stomach, and then he gently turns me around so he can wash my back. When he finishes he moves on to my hair.

He pulls me even closer and begins to massage my scalp as he works the soap into my hair.

"I want to call you by a name," I murmur, my eyes closed as I try not to get lost in the delicious feeling of his fingers in my hair.

"I do not remember my name," he admits, a hint of sadness in his voice. "I suppose I'm not really the same man that wore that name anymore anyway."

"Friends call me Letta," I say. "Or friendly people I guess. The people in town who don't think I'm some crazed Satan worshiper. I guess they think it sounds more fun—cuter than Arletta. Easier to swallow and stomach. If I sound normal then they can more easily convince themselves that I am. But I like being Arletta."

"Arletta is a beautiful name," he says.

"Thank you," I say softly. "I could choose to go by Letta, but I don't. I choose to be Arletta."

I look over my shoulder, wishing he had eyes I could gaze into. But at least the disturbing sight of his headless body has lessened. I am beginning to feel his beauty in the way he can feel mine.

"Choose a name," I say.

"You choose one for me, my sweet thing."

I bite my lip and think for a moment.

"Hesse."

He laughs softly, it's a happy sound.

"Alright then. Lean back, let me rinse your hair."

I do as he says and once my hair is clean he pulls me close once more, my back against his chest.

"Want to try something?" He murmurs, his voice brushing against one ear while his finger toys with the other.

30

"What?" I say around a sigh I'm failing to swallow.

I see him reach out and pluck one of the floating candles out of the air.

I try to shift away from him.

"You want to burn me?"

He tightens his hold on me.

"No," he says. "Hold out your arm."

I hesitate.

"My sweet Arletta," he says, still stroking the spot behind my ear, "the next time you fail to obey me, I *will* punish you."

I hold out my arm.

"Good girl," he murmurs.

Then he tips the candle to the side and lets the wax drip onto my skin. I hiss softly from the quick, hot sting, but once it settles I realize the pain provides a familiar kind of pleasure. Like how it felt to be spanked by him.

"Keep going," I whisper.

"Lean forward."

I do as he says and he begins to drip the wax in various spots along my back. My gasps get louder as the hot sensation causes my arousal to rise higher and higher.

"Now your breasts," he commands, spinning me around.

"I don't know," I whisper. They seem far too sensitive for this.

"Don't disobey now, my sweet thing," he says softly. "You're doing so well."

"Okay," I say.

He drips some wax onto my chest and it slides across my left nipple. I gasp and move away.

"Too much," I say.

He tosses the candle aside, the flame sputtering out in the water, and reaches for me.

"Are you going to punish me now?"

"Yes," he says. "But do not worry. You will like it."

"Then it's not much of a punishment is it?"

He laughs.

"It will be painful, but I shall make the pain sweet. Come, *my* sweet thing."

He lifts me from the water and carries me back to the bedroom but instead of laying me down on the bed, he sets me down on my feet.

"Put your hands on the bedpost."

I obey and suddenly thick, black rope winds itself around my wrists, fastening me tightly to the post.

"Hesse," I ask nervously.

He grips the back of my neck and presses his fingers into my skin.

"Trust me, Arletta."

He nudges my legs further apart then grabs my hips and tilts them so that my ass is sticking out.

"You're going to spank me, aren't you?"

"Yes, Arletta."

I am quiet for a moment and he is still. He can sense that there's more I want to say.

"Hard?"

"Yes. Have you ever been spanked before?"

I shake my head.

He begins to drag his nails lightly across my ass and I inhale sharply yet again.

"Did you like how it felt when I spanked you between your legs earlier?" He asks.

I nod again.

"Use your words, Arletta."

"Yes. I liked it."

"Then let me give you more."

"Okay," I gasp as he digs his fingernails deep into my ass.

I can feel my blood rush to the surface of my skin, hot and intense. Like everything else he's done to me tonight, I'm surprised by how much I enjoy such an aggressive sensation.

"Ready, my Arletta?"

"Yes, Master."

He spanks me. Harder than he did earlier this evening when he brought me here.

I cry out and my body leans forward on instinct. He responds to this by wrapping one arm around my waist to keep me still, while the other hits my ass over and over again until my legs are shaking and tears are wetting my cheeks from the overwhelming effect of the combination of soothing rubs and painful spanks have wrought upon my body.

"Hesse," I rasp.

He turns me around to face him, my hands still tied to the bedpost.

"Are you done?" I ask, not entirely sure I want him to be.

"How can I be? The front of your body isn't red at all."

His words send a thrum through my body, my skin already itching to be beautifully abused by his hands.

I can sense his sensual smile (that only exists in theory) at the slight motion of me tilting my hips just a bit closer to him.

He pushes my legs even further apart and begins to spank my pussy and inner thighs until I'm trembling and screaming. When I'm close to climaxing he unties me with a wave of his hand, then hoists me into the air. I wrap my legs around his back as he slams his cock deep inside me.

He fucks me roughly against the bedpost and I bury my head

into his shoulder, moaning with each powerful thrust.

"Arletta," he says, his voice raspy in the air.

"Master," I murmur.

He thrusts as hard as he can and we both come together.

I feel so sated.

I feel so strangely at peace.

He slowly pulls out of me and lowers me back down. He keeps his hands wrapped around my waist so I don't fall on my shaking legs; tired from being so thoroughly fucked.

"I wish I could kiss you," I say softly, looking up at his neck.

"Nothing would bring me more joy," he says, cupping my cheek in his hand.

"Why...why are you like this? Why don't you have your head? If you're a ghost I don't understand why your body doesn't look—"

"I'm not really a ghost, my sweet thing," he interjects. "I'm something else. An employ of Death. If I had truly moved on and left the mortal realm behind then I would have my proper body back. But as this in-between man, I am now Death has granted me the Jack-O-Lantern to see in your world when I ride out. But otherwise, my body looks the way it did when I died."

"What if you had your head? The skull? Would that work?"

"Perhaps. But it doesn't matter, I was surely buried in an unmarked grave. And I can only ride out on All Hallows' Eve."

"Too busy punishing the wicked to go to the library and research witch graves I guess," I say.

He laughs and pulls me into an embrace.

"Yes, that's right."

We take another bath to wash the wax and bits of dried blood from my backside and Hesse gently caresses each lovely blooming bruise across my backside. I never thought I would find such rough sexual pleasure so intoxicating but he has awakened something new in me.

Something ravenous.

Something primal.

I open my arms wide to welcome it.

After the bath, he carries me to bed and I remind him that I can walk but he just laughs and ignores me. We settle into the large, cloud-soft bed together and he wraps his arm around my stomach as he pulls my back against his chest. He begins to stroke my hair and it lulls me to sleep.

* * *

I wake before Hesse does. There are no windows in his bed chamber but my morning bird body can sense the risen sun out in the mortal realm.

I look down at his resting body. Odd to think how I'm no longer at all unsettled by his arguably ghastly form.

I believe he truly can see my soul.

And I think I can see his.

Which is why I know what I need to do.

I get out of bed and tiptoe out to the foyer where I find my nightgown and cardigan where I discarded them last night. I slip into them but leave my panties on the floor.

I creep outside to where Hesse's shadow steed stands outside the manor.

"Hello," I say to the beast. "Can you understand me?"

The horse nods.

Magic, Death realm horse, nice.

"Can you take me back to Sleepy Hollow? I promise I will return."

The Veil is only thin until the sun has fully risen in the mortal realm. It is dawn there now. You won't have enough time to cross back over.

Okay, so the magic death horse can audibly think too. Nothing weird about that. No siree.

"I know," I tell the horse.

Master won't be happy.

"I know that too."

Very well, the horse says. *It's your neck on the line.*

"Ha ha," I say, then climb up.

Six

The Almost Ending

I was a fool to think a brilliant, beautiful, soulful creature like her could love a mangled monster like me.

Maybe I will collect her soul next All Hallows' Eve. Dead or alive.

Seven

Faith, Dear Sir

Six Months Later

I t took months of research and badgering less than thrilled folks in town to speak with me. But I finally found it.

"I don't know how much help I'm going to be," Samantha Waverly says from beside me. She taps her shovel against mine. "I have pretty weak arms."

"It rained last night," I say, "this is the best time to dig. We have all night."

"You did some witchy shit to make sure no one finds us, didn't you?"

"You bet I did."

Samantha smirks. She's become a good friend since I came back to town last Halloween to find her on my doorstep in the fresh morning light. She jumped up when she saw me coming. *I had a feeling,* she had explained, looking nervous and embarrassed, *that something had happened to you.* Then she reached into her jacket pocket and pulled out one of my tarot cards. The Two of Cups. She shifted nervously before speaking again: *the reading was about you. Wasn't it?* I just smiled at her and said: *You're a witch, aren't you Samantha Waverly?*

And she nodded.

I should've known.

Herbs are their own kind of magic.

And everyone knows that a witchy best friend is the *best* person to enlist in helping you desecrate a hidden mass grave full of the bodies of witchcraft trial victims.

"How are you going to know which head is his?" She asks.

"Do you think there's a lot down there?"

She shrugs.

"Well I haven't heard of anyone else being decapitated for witchcraft, I thought that was a vampire thing but I guess good old Sleepy Hollow liked to mix their monster hunting lore. So if they punished your lover that way, then they probably punished others the same way."

"Crap," I mutter. I kind of just thought there would be one lone loose head down there rolling around and ready for me to rescue it.

"Maybe it will...I don't know, call out to you?" Samantha suggests.

"Did they bury them naked?" I ask.

"Wow, Arletta," she says, "you just keep getting kinkier."

I smack her shovel with mine and she laughs.

"Maybe he was buried in the same clothes I saw him in on Halloween."

"Ohhhh," she says. "Good call. Let's get to digging."

"Wow, Samantha, never knew you got so enthusiastic about grave robbing."

"First of all we're only partially grave robbing and second of all my WiFi is down so this is a more entertaining way to spend the night."

I laugh and she does too. It's a sweet sound. I'll miss it. Of course, I'll be able to visit every Halloween.

(Assuming he'll take me back after I abandoned him.)

We dig.

About twenty minutes later we start finding skeletons. Half an hour later we find a body whose clothing I recognize.

And a skull nearby.

* * *

All Hallows' Eve Reprise

I reach the bridge, clutching the skull wrapped in a silk scarf Samantha gave me close to my chest.

He still wants me, I tell myself over and over again, because I cannot accept any other truth.

Let it hereby be known that I, Arletta Harrington, may not have believed in Death, or soul mates, or destiny, but I have always believed in love.

True, pure, passionate love.

No matter how strange and unusual that love may be.

So I cross the bridge.

* * *

You're back, mortal, the magic death horse says as I approach Hesse's bone manor.

"I told you I would be."

Mortals lie.

I shrug.

"Is he home?"

The sun has not yet set in the mortal realm, his ride does not begin until midnight.

"Okay, cool. Talk to you later."

Talk to you later, Arletta.

I wave to the horse and walk to the manor's front door. I take a deep breath and enter.

I find the foyer empty.

The bed chamber is empty too.

The bath is not.

He sits there, facing away from me, his body glistening with water as he leans back against the ledge.

I take a few, silent steps into the room, holding the silk-wrapped skull in front of me.

"Master."

I see him stiffen. Then he stands up slowly and turns to face me. I can feel him. I can feel the way he sees me. I can *almost* see his soul.

I unwrap the scarf and let it fall to the floor.

"Arletta," he whispers.

I hold his skull out to him.

"I want—" I say, taking another step closer to him. "—to kiss you."

41

He reaches out and gently places his hands on the skull, but not fully grasping it and taking it from me.

"You left me," he says.

"I know," I say. "I'm sorry. I went to—"

"—get this?" He asks, softly, his voice sounding full of awe and disbelief.

"I'm here now," I insist, pushing the skull into his hands.

He takes it from me gingerly and holds it out before himself.

"Forever?" He asks me, his voice ragged with want.

I nod.

"Yes, Hesse. Forever."

A pause.

Silence.

Fear starts to grip me. He's going to turn me away. Or kill me. He doesn't want me anymore. I fight the urge to let my tears from months of worry and stress fall when he finally speaks.

"Alright then, my Arletta."

He sets the skull on his shoulders.

As soon as it meets his ghostly body it is no longer a skull.

I gasp as I look into the eyes of the love of my life. They are a deep, beautiful blue, like the ocean on a clear summer day. His hair is red and fiery, full of curls that fall in his face. And my god his smile is the most beautiful thing I have ever seen.

He has tears in his eyes.

So do I.

"Arletta."

He moves forward and so do I. I jump into his arms and he holds me tight.

"Arletta," he says again.

My name sounds like a song on his tongue. In his voice. His real, true voice, rich with his Hessian German accent. I lean

42

back to look into his eyes again. He smiles and I don't think any painter in this world has ever captured anything more magnificent.

"I love you, Arletta," he says.

I lean down and press my mouth to his.

I kiss him for the first time and I can finally feel his soul the way he can feel mine. He is mine as much as I am his.

He presses his tongue to the seam of my lips and I part them to allow him to invade my mouth, fucking me with his tongue. I moan and tangle my hands in his glorious red hair.

He carries me to the bed and lays me down but as he moves to get on top of me I push him down onto his back and straddle him. He laughs joyously and I smile back at him. I reach between us and position his cock up to my entrance.

"I'm not going to be gentle the first time."

He laughs again. "Do your worst, my sweet thing."

I grin and then I lower myself down onto his cock, moaning from the rich, thick pleasure of him filling me up. He digs his fingers into my hips and bucks his own up against me, a beautiful groan escaping his lips.

I begin to move back and forth, riding him like he's my very own valiant steed. He sits up and wraps his arms around me and helps in moving me up and down; slamming me onto his cock over and over again until we're both enraptured by each other's moans of passion.

"Come for me, my sweet thing. My Arletta."

"Yes, Master," I gasp.

We both come together once more and it is euphoric.

But just when I think we're done for the evening he crawls on top of me and grins wickedly.

"What are you doing?"

He begins to crawl down my stomach, planting kisses and love bites across my skin.

"Something I have wanted to do rather terribly since the moment I first laid eyes on you."

He makes his way to the tuft of hair above my sex and I gasp as he uses his fingers to spread my folds as wide as he can and dips down to drag his tongue through them; up and down the length of my pussy.

I arch my back and cry out as he begins to fuck me with his tongue, flicking and biting at my clit with every other swipe of his tongue.

I really do prefer him with a head, I must admit.

"You taste delicious, my sweet thing," he murmurs as he nuzzles into my folds and licks me thoroughly once more.

I tilt my hips up, practically riding his face as he pushes his tongue in and out of my cunt, pinching my clit as he does and I finish with a scream so loud it could wake the dead.

He crawls back up to me and kisses me with a feverish passion, the taste of my sex on our lips.

We collapse into a tangled heap of limbs and panting breaths. He places his hand over my heart so that he can feel it beating. I shift closer to him and wrap myself around his torso, swinging my leg over his hips. He smiles (and I swear the whole goddamn world stops) and hooks a hand under my knee to pull me back on top of him, this time resting flat on his chest.

I trace my finger down his sharp jawline and lean forward to kiss him again. We kiss each other for a small eternity that seems to last the entire night.

The first Halloween in centuries where The Headless Horseman didn't head out for his nighttime ride.

He grips the back of my head firmly, knotting his fingers in my hair, and kisses me so thoroughly that my lips are red and swollen.

We break the kiss for a moment and I gaze again into his beautiful eyes.

"What is it?" He asks.

I smile and answer:

"I love you too."

THE END

Acknowledgments

Thank you to my wonderful friend River Meade! They designed this stunning cover you hold in your hands (or see on your device), they cheered on this story, and filled me with so much confidence and excitement in this project. It would not be the story it has become without her. Thank you to my beautiful editors Marcia L. Ruiz-Olguín and Elizabeth Zarb. Thank you to my mother who when I told her I was going to write an erotic novella titled Riding The Headless Horseman replied "THAT'S A GREAT IDEA!" And was 100% serious (my mom is better than your mom, sorry I don't make the rules). Thank you to my beta readers River (@darkwingdyke), Emily (@balladsandbookends), Annaka (@annakahart), And Maisie Dickson (@maisie_dicksonsws) and thank you to my lovely Ko-Fi supporters AH, Juniper, Maisie, Em, Milky, and BCE. Lastly, thank you to YOU the reader. Thank you for embarking on this absurd, sexy story. I hope you enjoyed it. Happy Halloween (if you're not reading this at Halloween time that's okay, Halloween is a state of mind).

About the Author

Molly Likovich is the author of various monster romances, poetry, and the occasional play. She has a BA in Creative Writing from Salisbury University, and her poems and short stories have appeared in numerous literary magazines. She is the head of the virtual theatre troupe The Bard Coven, and she has a TikTok audience of over 70K viewers. To learn more visit mollylikovich.com

Other Works

Library of Teeth

Be Terrible: A Holiday Monster Romance

Not a Myth

The Willow's Silence

The Fable of Wonderland

Loved Alone